This edition published by Parragon in 2012
Parragon
Chartist House
15-17 Trim Street
Bath BA1 1HA, UK
www.parragon.com

Edited by Samantha Crockford
Designed by Pete Hampshire
Production by Emma Fulleylove

ISBN 978-1-4454-7393-2

Printed in China

STORYBOOK COLLECTION

PaRragon

Bath • New York • Singapore • Hong Kong • Cologne • Delhi
Melbourne • Amsterdam • Johannesburg • Shenzhen

THIS BOOK BELONGS TO

· ·

CONTENTS

THE UNLUCKY LADYBIRD

"Silvermist!" Iris, a garden-talent fairy, called out as she rushed up with an armful of chrysanthe-poppies. "Thanks for waiting!"

Silvermist, a water talent, sat up in her canoe. The fairies were having a picnic on an island not far from Pixie Hollow. Silvermist had promised Iris she would bring the flowers there for her.

Iris carefully put the chrysanthe-poppies in the canoe.

"See you there!" Silvermist said, paddling off.

"Moving a bit slowly today, sweetheart?" asked Vidia, landing lightly on the end of the canoe.

"Hi, Vidia. Are you going to the picnic?" Silvermist asked.

Vidia laughed. "Goodness, no."

"How are my flowers?" Iris shouted from the water's edge.

"Flowers? Is that what those weeds are?" Vidia asked, leaning over to look.

Suddenly the canoe tipped... and Vidia fell backwards into the water!

Vidia waved her arms in alarm. A crowd of fairies flew over and helped her up.

The canoe bumped against the shore. Silvermist climbed out and hurried to Vidia, who sat dripping on the beach. "Are you all right?"

"I'm f-f-fine," Vidia snapped. "Next time don't rock the boat." She shook her long, wet ponytail and stormed off.

Silvermist felt terrible about what had happened. But she was still enjoying the picnic.

After lunch, Beck, an animal-talent fairy, suggested they play spots and dots. Beck gathered dozens of ladybirds that wanted to play. The ladybirds had ten seconds to hide. Then the fairies had to find as many of them as possible and count their dots. The fairy with the highest score won.

When it was time to search for the ladybirds, Silvermist checked every hiding place she could think of. She found one ladybird in a bush. Another was hiding in a nest. Then she spotted an unusual-looking ladybird. It was milky white, and its dots were white, too.

To her surprise, the white ladybird hopped on her head.

"Hey!" Silvermist called out to the other fairies. "Do I get extra points if a ladybird finds *me*?"

Silvermist's friends gathered around her.

"White ladybirds bring bad luck!" Iris gasped.

A hush fell over the picnic. Fairies were superstitious creatures. They believed in wishes, charms and luck – both good and bad.

Silvermist shook her head, trying to get the ladybird to fly away. But it wouldn't.

"Here, let us help." Beck and Fawn, another animal-talent fairy, lifted the ladybird and carried it to a tree.

"Let's play fairy tag," Firu, a light talent, suggested. She looked around at the fairies. Finally she tapped Silvermist. "You're it!" she said.

Silvermist waited while her friends scattered. Then she flew after Beck.

"Yoo-hoo, what about me?" Fawn called.

Silvermist turned to chase Fawn – and crashed into a tree trunk.

"Ouch!" she cried, fluttering to the ground.

"Well, that was a little strange," Silvermist said.

"Strange? It's terrible! You're cursed, Silvermist!" Iris said, backing away.

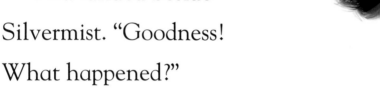

Fira landed beside Silvermist. "Goodness! What happened?"

"It was just an accident," Silvermist said.

"I don't think so," said Vidia, who was stuck on the island until her wings dried. "A fairy needs to be pretty unlucky to fly into a tree."

Everyone stared at Silvermist. She couldn't believe it. Were they really scared of a harmless ladybird?

"There's no such thing as bad luck," she told the other fairies. "I'm not going to pay attention to this crazy superstition and neither should you."

"Any fairy could have a little flying accident," Silvermist told herself later. Still, she knew her friends thought she had bad luck and that she was cursed.

But I don't believe it, Silvermist thought as she flew back to the Home Tree. Maybe she could help the cooking fairies get ready for dinner.

"Hi, Dulcie," she said, flying into the kitchen. "Anything I can do?"

Dulcie quickly shook her head. "We're all set. You don't even have to come inside," she said.

"Just let me fill the water pitchers," Silvermist said, landing at the water pump. She caught the flowing water and sent it streaming over Dulcie's head into a jug.

At that moment, Vidia swept into the kitchen. "I was just flying past and saw you here, Silvermist. Any more accidents?"

"Nope." Silvermist shot another stream into the pitcher. "Not one."

But when she turned, her wing brushed against a jug. The jug tipped over and fell against another jug. Silvermist tried to catch them, but she wasn't fast enough.

Water splashed onto the honey buns and into the walnut soup. Fairies rushed around the room with moss mops and towels.

"Hmmm," Vidia said smugly. "Looks like dinner might be late tonight."

That evening during dessert, Silvermist reached for the sugar bowl and knocked over the pepper. "Oops!"

"Oh!" Iris moaned. "That's bad luck, too!"

"Quick! Toss some over your left shoulder!" Fira urged.

Silvermist threw a handful of pepper over her shoulder... right into the face of a serving talent! He sneezed and the platter of pudding he was carrying crashed to the floor.

Maybe I *do* have bad luck, Silvermist thought sadly as the fairies and sparrow men filed quietly out of the Tea Room. Maybe the curse is real!

The next morning, Silvermist felt better. She flung open her window to let in the fresh air.

Chirp! A cricket hopped onto a branch outside her window and began to sing.

Silvermist smiled. If she were really unlucky, would a cricket sing her a special song?

But when she flew into the courtyard, she found out there had been a songbird concert – and that she had missed it.

Silvermist felt tears coming on. She was the kind of fairy who flew into trees. And tipped over water pitchers. And missed songbirds. No doubt about it – Silvermist was unlucky.

Word spread quickly that Silvermist had missed the concert.

"I told you! She's cursed!" Iris said, fluttering from fairy to fairy.

Rani called the worried fairies to attention. "I have an announcement. There will be a waterball tournament tomorrow. All water talents are invited to show their skills!"

"I'm sure Silvermist won't be taking part due to a severe case of bad luck," Vidia said.

Silvermist frowned. "Vidia is mistaken," she said, smiling at Rani. "I will be there."

The water talents cheered. Silvermist knew she had done the right thing. But still, she was worried.

"I just know something's going to go wrong," she told Fira as they left the courtyard.

"Let's visit the library," Fira suggested. "It might give us an idea."

The two fairies found lots of books on superstition. Silvermist learned that the curse of the white ladybug was a very powerful one.

But she also found out she could undo the curse with a good-luck charm.

The fairies made a list of things they could do to bring good luck.

"Find a five-leaf clover," Silvermist said. But that would take too long. "What about 'collect a swan feather'?"

"Let's try it!" Fira said.

The fairies flew to Crescent Lake. "Look!" Silvermist cried. "Two swans!" The swans floated past a nest built on the bank.

The fairies flew to the nest. "No feathers," Silvermist said.

"That's okay." Fira flapped her wings. "We'll go after them. They're bound to lose one feather!"

Silvermist started to follow Fira, but her dress snagged on a twig. Suddenly she heard a flutter.

"Fira?" she called.

But it wasn't Fira. It was an angry black swan!

Silvermist was able to tear her dress free, and she and Fira flew safely back to Pixie Hollow. But I still don't have a good-luck charm, she thought worriedly.

The next day, Silvermist arrived bright and early at the contest field. Queen Clarion sat on a colourful mat near the targets. Fairies and sparrow men milled about, talking and laughing.

"Water talents, take your places behind the line," the queen announced. "You each have five tries to hit the target."

Each of the water talents took a turn until only Silvermist was left. She scooped up the water and made her throw.

The waterball soared through the air towards the target... and hit Queen Clarion in the face!

Silvermist could barely look. What would the queen do?

To Silvermist's amazement, Queen Clarion laughed!

"Well, that cooled me off!" said the queen. Soon everyone was laughing – even Silvermist.

Then Silvermist noticed a five-leaf clover. "Everyone, look!" she called.

"Five-leaf clovers are magic – and lucky!" Fira said.

Silvermist picked the clover and tucked it behind her ear.

"It's still your turn, Silvermist," Vidia reminded her.

Silvermist faced the fairies. "I'm not sure if I had bad luck or just a few bad days," she told her friends. "But I do know that if you believe you'll have bad luck, you will."

She turned back to the target and tossed her waterball. *Splash!*

"Bull's-eye!" cried Fira.

"You broke the curse!" Iris said.

Silvermist grinned. "Looks like today is my lucky day!"

ROSETTA'S
BASHFUL BLOOM

"Rosetta! Catch!" Tinker Bell called out.

The garden talent looked up just in time to catch a brand-new watering can.

"Thank you, Tink!" Rosetta called. Her friend waved and flew off. Rosetta quickly filled her new watering can. Her old one had just sprung a leak, so she was glad to have another!

The fairies of Pixie Hollow were very busy preparing to bring autumn to the mainland.

Silvermist and the water-talent fairies were learning how to make ice crystals for the first frost. The winter fairies had offered to teach them! Working with another talent always excited Silvermist.

Iridessa and the other light-talent fairies were collecting bright, clear autumn sunlight in bottles.

And Fawn was practising new bedtime stories to tell the baby animals that were going to sleep through the long winter.

As a garden talent, Rosetta usually had to do more work to prepare for the spring and summer seasons on the mainland than for the autumn. But this autumn, she was as busy as her friends.

There was the usual work in her own garden, such as watering the tulips, singing to the tiger lilies and complimenting the roses. But on top of all that, Rosetta had a new flower to take care of.

Not too long ago, the Minister of Autumn had given Rosetta a seed wrapped in beautiful red fabric. He wanted her to grow a special autumn flower to bring to the mainland.

"This seed will grow an autumn daisy," the minister had said. "I know you'll take good care of this little flower, Rosetta."

"You just leave it up to me!" Rosetta had told the minister with a grin and a wink. "Little daisy-pie and I are going to be best buds, aren't we? Get it? Best... *buds?*"

The trip to the mainland was right around the corner. Rosetta should have been happy about bringing the new flower over. But actually, she was a little worried.

The autumn daisy had sprouted quickly. It had grown into a dull green plant with a single yellow flower bud. The plant wasn't tall, and its leaves weren't shiny. It wasn't exactly strange looking, but it wasn't very pretty, either.

It was the most ordinary plant Rosetta had ever raised.

Rosetta was known for growing amazing plants. Her flowers were gorgeous. They were not ordinary.

She let out a frustrated sigh.

"I must be doing something wrong," she said.

Rosetta ran through her "Happy Plant Checklist":

Water? Check.

Sunlight? Check.

Rich soil? Check.

Praise? Double check.

Rosetta always praised her plants. She told her forget-me-nots that they were bluer than the summer sky. She told her roses that they were redder than the setting sun. The flowers seemed to perk up at Rosetta's kind words.

But flattery didn't seem to work with the autumn daisy. When Rosetta said, "You smell sweeter than honey," it wilted before her very eyes. And when she told it, "Your blossom will outshine the moon and stars," she could have sworn its single flower bud closed up even tighter.

At this rate, the daisy was never going to be ready for the trip to the mainland. Rosetta didn't want to let the Minister of Autumn or her little bloom down!

That night, Rosetta lay awake in her rose-petal bed. She stared at the ceiling. What was she doing wrong? Why was this one plant so drab when all her other plants were bright and cheerful?

She had been working hard to think up new compliments for the autumn daisy, but each one only seemed to make it sadder.

"Tomorrow I'll figure this out," she promised herself. "I'm going to find a way to make the autumn daisy the prettiest autumn-blooming flower the mainland has ever seen."

When the pink light of dawn peeked into Rosetta's bedroom the next morning, she was dressed and ready for the day.

"First," she decided, "I'll see what Iridessa thinks."

Rosetta found her friend in a field of goldenrod. The light fairies were using jars to collect the rays of sunlight that bounced off the golden flowers.

"Tonight, we're going to mix the sunlight with moonlight," Iridessa explained. "This autumn, the mainland will have the most golden harvest moon ever!"

Rosetta told Iridessa all about the autumn daisy. "I've tried everything," she said, sighing.

"It sounds like you have," Iridessa agreed. "How can I help?"

"Will you come and look at it, Dess?" Rosetta asked. "Maybe you can tell if it's getting enough sunlight."

"Of course!" Iridessa said. She placed the lid on her jar. Then she flew off to Rosetta's garden.

Iridessa knelt down beside the plant.

"Let's see," the light talent said. She held her hands out over the plant and closed her eyes. A moment later, she opened them again.

"It is getting enough sun. I can feel the energy stored in its leaves," Iridessa said.

"Hmm," Rosetta replied. "Maybe it isn't getting enough water. Let's go ask Silvermist!"

She and Iridessa flew over to the babbling brook, where Silvermist was catching up on the latest fairy gossip. She agreed to take a look at the little flower.

The moment Silvermist saw the plant, she shook her head. "It's getting plenty of water," she said.

"Well," Rosetta said, "if it doesn't need sunshine, and it doesn't need water, then what does it need?"

Just then, they noticed Tink and Fawn flying nearby. Rosetta waved them over.

When Fawn saw the autumn daisy, she shrugged. "It's a little small, but it looks all right," she said.

Tink agreed with Fawn. "The plant seems fine. Are you sure there really is something wrong with it?"

"Just look at it!" Rosetta said impatiently. "It's so... so *ordinary*!"

Her friends looked at one another doubtfully.

"And here, watch this!" Rosetta said.

She knelt down in front of the flower. Then she smiled at the plant and said, "When your leaves sway in the breeze, even the most graceful birds look clumsy."

The daisy quivered a bit and then curled itself into a little lump.

Fawn gasped. "It looks like the saddest snail ever," she said. "I've never seen such a bashful little thing."

"See!" Rosetta cried. "Any other plant would be glowing after praise like that." She shook her head. "It's no use. I'm going to have to tell the Minister of Autumn that I failed."

With that, she flew straight to the Autumn Forest.

Rosetta was sorry that the mainland wouldn't get its new plant that autumn. She felt bad about disappointing the minister. But she felt even worse about failing the autumn daisy.

When Rosetta arrived at the minister's chambers, she told him the whole story.

"It's getting enough water and enough light," Rosetta said. "And I've been paying it plenty of compliments, too. But they just make things worse! The other day I told the autumn daisy that its leaves were as soft as a kitten's ear, and it actually tried to hide behind a poppy plant."

"Rosetta, autumn plants are not like spring or summer plants," the minister said. "Because winter is so close, autumn flowers aren't showy or bright like most other flowers. And they can be very, very shy."

"Fawn did say the daisy was bashful," Rosetta said.

"I think all your flattery may be *embarrassing* the daisy," the minister said.

Rosetta gasped. "That's not what I wanted to do!" she said. "I just wanted to make the little daisy-pie happy."

The minister smiled. He gathered some autumn plants in his hands. "Autumn flowers are most happy when they blend into their surroundings," he said. "They work together with the other plants to make the world beautiful as they change colour."

When Rosetta got back to her garden, she sat beside the bashful daisy with a handful of autumn plants. "Little daisy-pie, look how well you blend in," she said. "Why, I think you made these other plants more beautiful."

Rosetta beamed as the autumn daisy stood up straighter. Its sturdy leaves bristled proudly. And its flower bud opened just a tiny bit.

"That's the spirit!" Rosetta quietly cheered. "How could I forget that working together makes everything brighter?"

The autumn daisy was finally ready to go to the mainland. And Rosetta had never been more proud of one of her blooms.

A MESSY MYSTERY

One morning, Tinker Bell flew to her workshop. She was eager to begin work on a set of tin measuring spoons. Dulcie, a baking-talent fairy, had dropped them off two nights before.

"The pinch-of-this spoon adds a pinch of *that*," Dulcie had told Tink. "And the add-a-dab spoon is adding a dollop instead. I ruined two batches of pumpkin muffins before I realized!"

Tink had assured her friend that she would get to the bottom of things.

"I bet the spoons need another layer or two of tin added," Tink said as she reached her workshop. With a burst of excitement, she flung open the door.

Tinker Bell gasped. "Blazing copper kettles!" she cried. Her workshop was a mess. Pots and pans and ladles were scattered all over the place.

But worst of all, the measuring spoons weren't where she'd left them. They were gone!

Tink took off for the kitchen. She wondered if Dulcie had come back for the spoons, thinking they were finished.

When she got there, Tinker Bell's mouth dropped open in surprise. "Dulcie, what's going on?" she asked.

"Someone made a mess!" Dulcie said. "And what's worse,

the gingerbread cupcakes I made are gone!"

Tinker Bell looked around. She spotted a trail of crumbs leading to the door of the Tea Room.

"Follow me!" she told Dulcie.

When Tink and Dulcie reached the Tea Room, they could hardly believe what they saw.

The Tea Room was a mess, too! And where the trail of cupcake crumbs ended, a trail of sugar began.

"Look!" Dulcie said. "The silver sugar shaker is missing. I put it here this morning!"

"Who is making this mess?" asked Prilla, a clapping talent. "Things are being turned upside down all over Pixie Hollow!"

"Someone has to solve this messy mystery," Tink said, pointing at the trail of sugar. "Prilla, will you help me?"

The sugar led out into the hall. It continued through the corridors and even went up the stairs!

"I can't believe this," Tink said as she and Prilla followed the sugary mess.

"Who do you think did it?" Prilla asked.

"I have no idea," Tink replied.

"Do you think it was a fairy?" Prilla continued. "Or maybe –"

"Beck!" Tink interrupted, coming to a halt. Prilla couldn't stop in time! She flew into Tink's back, and Tink stumbled forwards.

"What?" Prilla said.

Tink pointed. The two fairies had followed the trail of sugar from the Tea Room all the way to Beck's door.

Beck was an animal-talent fairy and one of Tink's good friends.

"What in Never Land would make Beck leave such a mess?" Tink wondered aloud.

The door to Beck's room
was open just a crack. Tink
and Prilla peered inside. Beck
was nowhere in sight, but Tink
spotted something glinting in
the sunlight streaming through
the window.

"Dulcie's measuring
spoons!" Tink cried.
She pushed open the door and
flew into the room. "Why does Beck have these?"

Prilla flew to another corner. "Look, Tink," she said, "the
sugar shaker."

Tink tugged on her hair. Could Beck really have taken the
spoons and the sugar shaker and made all those messes?

"Come on," Tink said, "we have to find Beck."

Tink and Prilla flew all over Pixie Hollow looking for Beck. She wasn't in the meadow with the field mice or at Havendish Stream with the water fairies.

Suddenly, Tink and Prilla spotted Bess, an art-talent fairy, fluttering around her studio. She looked upset.

"Look at this mess!" Bess cried when Tink and Prilla flew up. "My paints are all over the floor, and the cake I was painting has disappeared!"

Prilla comforted Bess while Tink looked around the studio.

Finally, Tink turned to Bess. "We'll get to the bottom of this messy mystery," she said. She gave her friend a warm smile. Then she took off. Prilla chased after her.

"Why would Beck make a mess in Bess's art studio?" Prilla asked.

"I don't know," Tink replied. The two fairies flew across a clearing and into a meadow filled with flowers.

"Why would she eat the cake Bess was painting?" Prilla asked.

"I don't know!" Tink snapped.

She watched Prilla shrink back in shock. Tink's glow flared orange with embarrassment. She knew Prilla was only trying to help. But she couldn't answer the questions the young fairy was asking!

"Prilla..." Tink began to apologize.

"Caught you!" Beck yelled as she flew up over some flowers.

Tink and Prilla jumped in surprise. "Beck!" Tink cried. "We've been looking all over for you."

"You have?" Beck asked. "Why?"

"There's a mess-maker in Pixie Hollow," Prilla said. "We followed the trail to you."

Beck began to laugh. "You've been following me, and I've been following *them*!" She pointed to the ground below where Tink and Prilla were hovering.

To Tink and Prilla's amazement, three baby hedgehogs came rolling out of the grass.

"We were playing hide-and-seek, but these little guys kept running away," Beck explained. "I tracked them all over Pixie Hollow before I finally caught up with them. I thought I could handle them on my own, but they're too much for just one fairy!"

"We can help," Prilla offered.

The three fairies worked together to build a space for the baby hedgehogs to play in.

"Now you can keep an eye on them while they have fun!" Prilla said, smiling.

"And best of all, we solved the messy mystery!" Tink said.

The fairies giggled and settled down to watch the hedgehog babies play.

A Fairy Flood

Rani, a water-talent fairy, hummed to herself as she hurried down the stairs. She was on her way to see her friend Tinker Bell. Rani wasn't looking where she was going. She didn't notice anything unusual until – *splash!*

Rani looked down. Her feet were covered with water!

"Oh, my!" Rani exclaimed as a teapot floated by. "The dishes are floating away!"

"The dishes aren't the only things floating away," Dulcie called out. The baking-talent fairy paddled towards Rani in a large pot. "All of Pixie Hollow is flooded!"

Before Rani could respond, she and Dulcie heard a fairy outside cry, "Help!"

"It sounds like someone is in trouble!" Rani said. She leaped into Dulcie's pot, and the two fairies paddled out of the door.

Lily, a garden-talent fairy, was trying to rescue a nest of baby birds that had fallen into the water.

"The nest is too heavy!" Lily cried. "Can you help me pull it in?"

Rani and Dulcie grabbed on to the branch Lily was holding. The three fairies pulled the chicks to safety.

Lily breathed a sigh of relief. "That was close," she said.

Rani nodded. She looked down at Dulcie's pot. It reminded her of something.

"Oh! I completely forgot – I have to go see Tink," Rani exclaimed. "Dulcie, can I borrow your pot and spoon?"

"Sure," Dulcie said.

Rani climbed into the pot.

"There's a dent in one of the handles," Dulcie called as Rani began to paddle away. "Would you ask –"

"Tink if she'll fix it? I'm sure she'd love to!" Rani waved and paddled off.

Rani arrived at Tink's workshop and knocked on the door. When Tink opened it, three fish leaped inside.

"These fish keep trying to jump into my pots and pans!" Tink cried. "I can't get any work done."

Rani spotted a shiny silver spoon. "How about a distraction?"

Tink dangled the spoon in the water. The fish swam around it.

Just then, Spring, a message-talent fairy, arrived. "Beck is looking for you," she told Rani. "She said it's urgent."

Rani climbed into Spring's boat. "Oh, Tink," she called back, "Dulcie's pot has a dent in the handle. Can you fix it for her?"

As Spring paddled away from Tink's workshop, Rani looked around. There was water as far as she could see!

Rani wondered where all the water was coming from. As a water-talent fairy, she knew her friends would be looking for her to help solve the problem.

Just then, Rani's friend Terence flew up. He was a dust-keeper. Rani thought she might be able to clear some of the water if she had a little more pixie dust.

Before Rani could ask, though, Terence said, "The pixie dust is all wet!"

Spring and Terence started talking about how the fairies would get around Pixie Hollow to do their work. Rani looked behind her and saw a group of water-talent fairies floating in leaf boats. One of the fairies reached out and touched the water. A fountain shot into the air. The other water talents began setting off fountains, too.

Rani was happy to see at least one talent group enjoying the flood. She wanted to stay and make fountains as well, but she knew Beck was waiting for her.

Spring and Terence were still discussing their plans, so Rani borrowed a leaf boat from another water talent. She paddled and paddled. It seemed there was no end to the flood of water! Suddenly, she heard someone calling her.

"Rani! Rani, there you are!"

Turning, Rani saw Beck riding on the back of a turtle.

"I know what's causing the flood!" Beck said. "Come on, I'll show you!"

The two fairies set off. Soon they arrived at a giant dam. The dam was keeping all the water in Pixie Hollow!

"Hello!" Beck said in Beaver. There was a splash, and three brown heads poked out of the water.

Beck chattered to the beavers. Then she turned to Rani. "They don't want to move," she said. "It took them a long time to find the perfect spot."

Rani thought for a moment. "Tell them I know a better spot!"

Beck told the beavers what Rani had said. They were quiet for a few minutes. Then they smacked their tails against the water.

"That's a yes!" Beck exclaimed.

The next day, the beavers moved their dam. The water began to flow away, and soon, the bright sun dried out Pixie Hollow. The green grass stood up tall. The flowers and plants stretched towards the sun's rays.

Rani walked around Pixie Hollow, helping any fairy she could. The pixie dust was dry, and Terence had given all the water-talent fairies an extra scoop so they could help clean up the floodwaters.

Tinker Bell was standing beside a leaf boat that was floating in a puddle. Rani noticed that her friend looked a little sad.

"What's wrong, Tink?" Rani asked. "Aren't you happy that Pixie Hollow is back to normal?"

"I guess so," Tink said with a sigh. "But I kind of miss those little fish. They were good company! And travelling by leaf boat was fun, too."

Rani smiled. Some other fairies had told her the same thing! "Come with me," she told Tink.

Rani led Tinker Bell
to a small cove off
Havendish Stream.
Tink gasped in delight!

There, fairies of all
talents paddled in leaf boats
and played with the fish.

Rani smiled. The flood
had made things difficult.
But she was glad to see
that the other fairies had
found ways to have fun with
water. She loved her talent
– and it was even better
when she could share it with her friends!

THE FAIRY CAMPOUT

Tinker Bell was resting on a bright red rose in the meadow. The tinker fairy had finished fixing all the pots and pans in her workshop. Now she was trying to plan her next adventure.

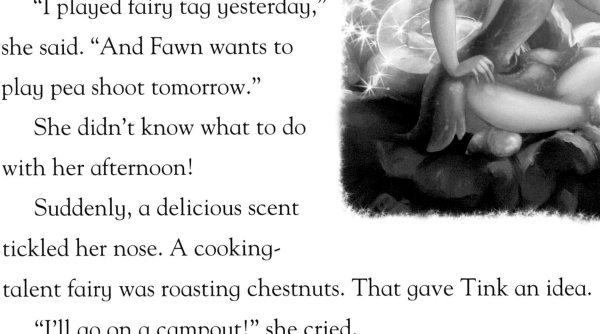

"I played fairy tag yesterday," she said. "And Fawn wants to play pea shoot tomorrow."

She didn't know what to do with her afternoon!

Suddenly, a delicious scent tickled her nose. A cooking-talent fairy was roasting chestnuts. That gave Tink an idea.

"I'll go on a campout!" she cried.

Tink flew to
the kitchen, where
she found her
friend Dulcie.

"I'm going on a
campout, and I need to
pack some food," she
told the baking talent.

"What's a campout?"
asked Dulcie.

"It's when you
make a home away from
home," Tink explained. "You pitch a tent, build a fire and cook
dinner, all outside under the stars."

Dulcie's eyes sparkled with excitement. "Can I come, too?"
she asked.

"Of course!" Tink exclaimed. "All fairies are welcome!"

Word of Tink's latest adventure quickly spread through Pixie Hollow. Fairies of all talents gathered leaf blankets and filled packs with their belongings.

Tink was waiting in the courtyard when everyone arrived. "Are you all ready?" she asked.

"Ready!" the fairies cried.

"Wait for me!" someone called out.

Tink turned around and saw Dulcie. She was carrying the biggest leaf pack Tink had ever seen.

"What's in that pack?" Tink asked.

"All my baking things!" Dulcie replied. "I can't imagine making a home away from home without them." Dulcie hefted the pack onto her back. "Are we ready to go?"

Tink shrugged. "We're all set," she said.

Tinker Bell flew up to the front of the crowd. "Let's go!" she called out.

The fairies zigzagged through the forest, looking for the perfect spot to set up camp. But they couldn't agree! The water fairies wanted to camp near Havendish Stream, while the forest fairies wanted to pitch their tents deep in the woods.

While the fairies discussed where to go, Dulcie set down her heavy pack. "Can't we just stop here?" she said, panting.

But Tink just shook her head. "I know the perfect place," she said. "Come on!"

Tink led the fairies to a pretty, sunlit clearing.

"It's close to the forest *and* the stream," she said. "And best of all, we can gaze up at the stars!"

"This *is* the perfect spot!" Prilla exclaimed. She set down her leaf pack and started to make camp. The other fairies joined her.

While Fira and the light talents made friends with the local fireflies, the other fairies pitched their tents in a circle. Then they built a giant campfire.

A group of forest-talent fairies set off to search the surrounding area for food. They returned to the camp with loads of berries, and even found some large chestnuts to roast over the fire.

"Brass buckles!" Tink exclaimed when she saw the chestnuts. "Those will be delicious."

As the sun set, the fairies began to prepare their dinner. A cooking talent roasted chestnuts over the fire. Prilla plucked ripe strawberries from the vine. The fairy campout was under way!

"Mmm," Rani said, taking another bite. "I've never had a better dinner."

Tink looked around the campsite. Everyone was having a wonderful time. But Tinker Bell couldn't help feeling that something was missing.

Suddenly, Tink snapped her fingers. "That's it!" she cried. "We need to tell campfire stories!"

The fairies gathered around the fire, and a storytelling talent began.

"Once upon a time, there was a ladybird who loved to dance –"

"No!" Tink interrupted. "Campfire stories have to be scary!"

"Scary?" Beck asked.

Tink smiled wide. "The scarier the better."

Suddenly, Beck flew up in front of the crowd. "I know a scary story!" she said. "It's about a snake with two heads."

Beck raised her arms, and the shadow of a two-headed snake appeared on the rock wall behind her.

"Oh, I know one, too!" Bess said. She leaped up from her seat and spread her arms wide. "It's about the ghost of an owl."

The fairies gasped. They took turns telling scary stories until everyone's wings shook.

Tink grinned. "I know the scariest story ever!"

She leaned close to the fire. "It's about a wicked, smelly... pirate!"

"Ooh." The fairies shuddered.

"And that's not all," Tink went on. "At the end of his arm was a huge metal hook!"

Clank! Crash!

"Ahh!" yelled the fairies. They jumped up from their seats and flew to their tents.

"What was that? Is someone out there? Why did we tell so many scary stories?" they asked all at once.

Tink quickly lit a torch. She crept quietly to the edge of the campsite.

Tink saw a shadow just beyond their camp. She flew closer and closer until she came face-to-face with...

"Dulcie!" Tink cried. "Where have you been?"

"I got lost," Dulcie said. She set down her heavy leaf pack. "It took me ages to find the campsite. Did I miss all the fun?"

Dulcie looked around in surprise. "Hey! Where is everyone?" she asked.

"They're hiding," Tinker Bell said. She told Dulcie about the scary stories they had told. "Beck told us about a two-headed snake, and Bess scared everyone with a story about a ghost owl. I was just starting my story when we heard a strange noise. Everyone went to hide in their tents."

"Well," Dulcie said, "I think I can fix that."

In no time at all, Dulcie had whipped up a special campfire cake. Even the most frightened fairies couldn't resist the delicious smell.

Tink helped Dulcie carry the cake to the centre of the campsite.

"I told you I couldn't make a home away from home without my baking things," Dulcie said as the fairies dug in.

Tink smiled. "The campout wouldn't have been as sweet without you, Dulcie."

LADY FAWN

"That was an incredible catch you made out there," Fawn declared. She smiled at the little grey field mouse trotting just behind her. "I've never had so much fun!"

The mouse lifted up a tiny muddy paw and gave Fawn a high five. He and his field-mouse friends had just finished an exciting game of fairy football.

Fawn loved being an animal-talent fairy. Her favourite part was playing rough-and-tumble games with her animal friends.

"What did you say?" Fawn asked, listening closely as the mice chattered away. "Sure! I would love to have another game soon!" she exclaimed.

Fawn giggled as the mice scampered home for lunch. She felt her stomach rumble. All that action on the field had worked up her appetite, too.

"Hmmm, maybe I'll see if there are any blueberry waffles left in the kitchen," she told herself as she flew into the centre of Pixie Hollow.

Fairies of all talents were busy in the courtyard. "I wonder what's going on," Fawn said.

Suddenly, Fawn's eyes widened. "The tea party! I forgot!"

A group of harvest fairies were carrying baskets of bright red strawberries. A light-talent fairy was adding rays of sunlight to a pink punch bowl. Several hummingbirds were working with decoration-talent fairies, draping tables with grapevines.

Two summer-rain fairies waved to Fawn.

"Welcome back!" she called to them.

The seasonal talents had just returned from bringing summer to the mainland. Queen Clarion and the Minister of Summer wanted to celebrate their hard work with a tea party for all the Never fairies and their animal friends.

"There you are," Rosetta said as she flew over to Fawn. As usual, the garden fairy looked beautiful. She was wearing a pink rose-petal dress and carrying a basket of bright blue forget-me-nots. "Let me guess," she said, taking in Fawn's muddy pants. "Leapfrog? Or was it hide-and-seek this time?"

Fawn laughed. "No, fairy football! You should play sometime, Rosetta. It's so much fun!"

"Not to mention dirty! I'm just not one for horsing around, Fawn. Can you imagine me all covered with mud?" Rosetta shivered, then gave her friend a warm smile. "In fact, I can't imagine *you* all prim and proper for the tea party!"

Rosetta stuck a blue forget-me-not into Fawn's hair. Then she flew off.

Fawn looked down at herself. She was covered with mud. Her pants had a rip above one knee. Prickly thistles were stuck to her hair.

Fawn wondered if Rosetta was right. She did like to horse around quite a bit. But was she *too* rough-and-tumble?

Fawn hurried home to get cleaned up. She slipped off her muddy shoes at the door. Then she opened her wardrobe.

There were a few pairs of trousers woven from dandelion fluff and some soft thistledown shirts. She knew these would be perfectly fine to wear to the tea party. But she wanted to be ladylike, too.

"And who better to help me than Rosetta!" she said.

She grabbed a set of clean clothes from her wardrobe and took off for Rosetta's house.

Rosetta was outside, scattering flower petals around her doorway when Fawn flew up.

"Rosetta," Fawn called out, "can you help me get ready for the tea party? I'd like to try to be... prim and proper. Like you!"

"Of course!" Rosetta said with a wide smile. She looked Fawn over from wingtip to toe. "First we have to clean off all that mud. Then we'll find you a dress. If you're going to be a lady, you should wear flowers, not weeds." She plucked Fawn's clothes from her hands and dropped them beside the door. Then she led her friend inside.

Fawn sat in front of Rosetta's dressing table. A ladybird was perched atop the mirror. "It's not hard to be a lady, is it?" Fawn asked.

The ladybird shook her head and grinned.

Fawn smiled. Then she settled back in her chair and let Rosetta get to work.

When Rosetta had pulled all the twigs and leaves from Fawn's hair, she smiled. "Now, there's a bubble bath with your name on it!" she said.

Fawn wrinkled her nose. Since the day she'd arrived, she'd disliked wing-washing time. But Rosetta wouldn't take no for an answer. She hurried Fawn into the tub. Then she poured lavender bubble bath into the warm water.

Once Fawn was cleaned up, Rosetta gave her a beautiful dress made of tulip petals.

"I'm not sure this is for me," Fawn said as she looked at her reflection in the mirror. "It's so… dainty."

"This is what ladies wear! The colour is perfect for you," Rosetta said. She tucked a pink pansy into Fawn's hair, which had been twisted into a fancy braid.

"You do want to be a lady, don't you?" the ladybird chimed in.

Fawn looked at the dress again. Then she nodded firmly. She took the soft lily slippers Rosetta offered and put them on. "If this is what it takes, I'll do it."

Now that Fawn *looked* like a lady, Rosetta wanted to teach her how to *act* like one, too. She took out two teacups and filled them with lemonade. She handed one to Fawn.

"Now, when you take a sip of tea, you want to hold your cup like so," Rosetta said. She wrapped her fingers around the handle but left her pinkie sticking up.

Fawn tried to hold the cup like Rosetta had shown her. But the teacup tipped, and she spilled lemonade down the front of her dress.

"Don't worry," Rosetta said. "Practice makes perfect. Let's try a curtsey next."

"A curtsey?" Fawn asked.

The ladybird stood up, held her wings out on both sides, and bent slightly forwards.

Fawn picked up her dress, crossed her left leg behind her right one and bowed. I did it! she thought – just before she lost her balance and tumbled to the floor.

After a few more unsuccessful tries, Fawn shrugged sadly. "Maybe I'm not meant to be a lady," she said. "I can only be me."

"That's it, Fawn!" Rosetta exclaimed. She took her friend's hand, and they flew to the meadow where Fawn had played football. A few of the field mice were still there.

Rosetta asked Fawn to explain to the mice what they were doing. The animals were eager to help!

Fawn practised walking gracefully by balancing a piece of bark on her head as she raced a mouse across the field. Then she tried another curtsy as she leaned down to touch noses with the smallest of the mice. He squeaked happily.

"Even Queen Clarion would be impressed," Rosetta said.

Finally, it was time for the tea party. All the fairies gathered in the courtyard dressed in their fairy best.

"Come on," Rosetta whispered to Fawn. "You're ready."

The two fairies approached the table where their friends were already sitting.

"Rosetta, who's your friend?" Tinker Bell asked. Then she looked more closely at Fawn. "Blazing copper kettles!" She gasped. "Fawn, is that you?"

"Fawn, you look lovely!" Silvermist said.

Fawn's glow flared brighter as her friends admired her dress and slippers.

Fawn told her friends how Rosetta had taught her to be a lady. As she came to the part where Rosetta had called on the field mice for help, she overheard something that made her ears perk up.

"We discovered a new game while we were on the mainland," a summer-rain fairy said. "The Clumsies call it baseball."

"A new game?" Fawn said, her eyes lighting up with excitement. The summer-rain fairy was already putting together two teams to try out the game.

Fawn looked down at her delicate petal dress. Then she turned to Rosetta with a hopeful smile. "What do you think?" she asked. "Can we play?"

Rosetta grinned. "Who says a lady can't have fun?"

Fawn sprang up from her seat. She was quickly followed by her friends. They listened carefully to the rules. Then, using acorn caps for bases, twigs for bats and acorns for balls, the Never fairies played their first-ever game of baseball.

"That was the best!" Fawn said after the game. She took a big bite of strawberry-seed cake.

The game had ended in a tie, and now all the fairies were enjoying the tea party.

Rosetta blew a stray piece of hair off her face. "I guess I don't always have to look perfect!"

"No one minds a little messiness now and then," Queen Clarion said as she came up behind them.

Fawn wiped a crumb from her flushed cheek. Then she passed a tray of blackberry tarts to Rosetta. "Would you like one?"

Rosetta winked. "After you, Fawn. Ladies first!"

VIDIA'S SNOWY SURPRISE

Vidia, a fast-flying fairy, loved to make fun of the other fairies' talents. She thought her talent made her better than everyone else.

One day, Vidia was so mean to a water fairy who was making fountains in Havendish Stream that the fairy began to cry.

Tinker Bell had seen the whole thing. She was furious!

"Someday you'll learn to appreciate another talent!" Tink yelled angrily.

Vidia just laughed. "Darling, that won't happen until it snows in Pixie Hollow," she said.

As Tink watched Vidia fly away, she swore she'd make Vidia be nice someday.

Word of Vidia's announcement quickly spread. The fairies were discouraged. They knew it would never snow in Pixie Hollow. And that meant Vidia would never change her mean ways.

A garden talent named Lily was tending her plants one day when she started to get cold. She shivered as she inspected her violets, and she shivered more when she checked on her bush with the bright red berries.

She rubbed her arms. "Why is it so chilly outside?" she said.

Just then, Lily noticed something strange falling from the sky. She caught one of the objects in her hand. It was cold and melted in her palm.

"Snow?" Lily said. She looked up at the sky. More crystal flakes fell around her.

"Lily!" Rosetta, another garden talent, called out to her. "Can you believe this? It's snowing in Pixie Hollow!"

Rosetta held out her hands to catch some flakes. They melted as quickly in her hands as they had in Lily's.

"I was by Havendish Stream with Rani when I saw the first flakes," Rosetta explained. "I flew here as fast as I could to make sure the gardens would be all right."

Lily nodded. It had never snowed in Pixie Hollow before, and the garden talents didn't know how their plants would fare.

"What in Never Land is going on?" Lily mumbled as she watched the snow fall.

Before long, a thin layer of white covered the ground. All the fairies came out to play in the snow.

Dulcie, a baking-talent fairy, caught a flake on her tongue. "Hmm," she said, "it's rather bland." She'd hoped the crystals would taste as sweet and sugary as they looked.

As the day went on, the snow continued to fall. Soon it came up to the fairies' knees. Everyone shivered, but they were so excited to see snow in Pixie Hollow that they didn't want to go inside.

Prilla scooped up a handful of snow and shaped it into a ball. With a twinkle in her eye, she tossed it at her friend Tinker Bell.

Tink laughed. "Watch out, Prilla!" she called. "I'll get you back!"

Soon, more fairies joined in the snowball fight. They laughed as they darted to and fro, trying to avoid the cold snowballs flying through the air.

Soon the fairies grew too cold to stay outside. The sewing talents set to work making hats and scarves and jackets. The shoemaking fairies made boots lined with dandelion fluff. The fairies loved their new fashions. And they kept them warm enough to play for hours!

By now, the snow was wing-deep. The art-talent fairies had discovered a new use for it!

"You can sculpt snow!" Bess told Tink. She'd built a perfect snow fairy, complete with wings made from sheets of frosted spiderwebs. The snow fairy looked remarkably like Tinker Bell!

At Havendish Stream, the water-talent fairies gathered together. The usually bubbling stream was now as smooth as glass.

Rani tapped her foot on the ice. "Look," she said. "It's hard and slippery, too." She stepped out onto the surface and started gliding across it.

"Come on!" she called to the others. "This is more fun than water-skating!"

The other water talents joined Rani. When they water-skated, they moved with the waves in the stream and splashed across the surface. But ice-skating was so fast!

"I feel like I'm flying!" a water talent cried. "But I'm not moving my wings at all. See? Not even a flutter!" She laughed as she raced across the ice.

Soon the other talents joined in. It wasn't quite as easy for them as it was for the water talents, but it wasn't hard, either. Everyone was having a great time.

Everyone... including Vidia! The fast-flying talents were racing down the hillsides on leaf sleds.

Vidia could never say no to a race. She zipped ahead of the others. "You can't catch me, darlings!" she shouted.

Terence, a dust-keeper fairy, pushed Tink along the snowy bank near the stream in a silver spoon.

"Faster, Terence, faster!" Tink cried.

Terence beat his wings as hard as he could. He pushed the spoon with all his might and then let go.

Tink went sailing down the snowy hill. "Blazing copper kettles!" she yelled. "I love snow!"

Tink slid to a stop beside Rani and Vidia.

"Well, Vidia," Rani said. "Now you have to be nice to all the other talents."

"Whatever do you mean?" Vidia asked.

"You said that you'd appreciate another talent when it snowed in Pixie Hollow," Tink reminded her.

Vidia sniffed. "I suppose I could... if I didn't have better things to do." And with a flip of her ponytail, she flew away.

Tink and Rani watched Vidia hop into her leaf sleigh.

"You know," Tink said, "I think Vidia does appreciate the other talents. Or she wouldn't be having this much fun!"

"And neither would we," Rani said. The two fairies smiled at each other and flew off to play in the snow with their friends.

The Diamond
Dust Snowflake

"Blazing copper kettles!" Tinker Bell exclaimed, a grin stretching across her face. "The Minister of Winter has asked me to make Queen Clarion a gift for this winter!"

Silvermist, a water-talent fairy, joined the other fairies gathered around Tink. "What are you going to make?" she asked.

Tink tugged on her hair. "That's the problem," she said. "I don't know!"

"You could make a sleigh," Rosetta suggested.

"Queen Clarion already has one," Tink replied.

"How about snowshoes?" asked Fawn.

Tink frowned. "That's not right for a queen."

Silvermist thought of the winter fairies with a pang of envy. Being a water talent was great. She loved going to the mainland at the end of each winter to scatter morning dewdrops and make bubbling fountains in newly thawed streams. But the winter fairies got to make *snow*, carefully crafting each and every flake.

Suddenly, Silvermist had an idea. "You could make the queen a special snowflake in honour of winter," she said.

Tink's wings fluttered so hard, she lifted into the air. "That's it, Sil!" she cried. "A special snowflake as pretty as lace. And I know just what to use!" Tink took off.

Silvermist spent the afternoon at Havendish Stream, practising her water fountains. But she thought about Tink and her snowflake for the queen the whole time.

All of a sudden, Tink flew towards her. "Silvermist! Look!" Tink called. In her hands was a rock-crystal bottle. "I wanted to show you, since it was your idea!"

Tink held out the bottle. It was filled with sparkling material. A ray of sunshine caught the bottle and it shone like a thousand stars. Silvermist blinked repeatedly – the light was so bright!

"It's diamond dust!" Tink said. "The mining talents found it. Won't it make a beautiful snowflake?"

"I just wish I knew more about snowflakes," Tink went on. "Diamond dust is so precious. What if I mess up?"

"You need to see more snowflakes, Tink," Silvermist said. "You should go to the Winter Woods! I'll go with you!"

"Yes!" Tink cried.

The Winter Woods were colder than cold. Tink and Silvermist bundled up in coats of finely spun spiders' thread. They put on boots and mittens lined with dandelion fluff. Finally the two fairies set off.

When they arrived in the Winter Woods, they were cheerfully greeted by the winter fairies. Silvermist flew in close to one of the fairies, who was shaping a snowflake. It looked like a frost blossom. Next to it was a large pile of finished snowflakes.

Silvermist took off her mitten and picked one up. The snowflake was a work of art. But unlike water, the snowflake in her hand was very cold. It made her shiver.

"Can you give me some pointers?" Tink asked the winter fairies. "I'm making a snowflake out of diamond dust for the queen!" She pulled the crystal bottle from her sleeve.

"You brought the diamond dust?" Silvermist asked, shocked.

Tink shrugged. "I didn't want to leave it at home."

The winter fairies eagerly taught Tink and Silvermist about the different snowflake shapes – the starburst, the rose and the sparkler. They even showed the two fairies how to carve each of the shapes.

"But it's not all work here in the Winter Woods," one of the fairies said with a grin.

"It's not?" Tink asked.

"No." The fairy giggled. Then, quick as a flash, she grabbed a handful of snow and threw it at Tink.

Tink wiped the snow from her face. Then she launched her own snowball at Silvermist! Soon, a full-on snowball fight raged.

Finally, worn out, Silvermist fell back into the snow. The other fairies were settling down, too. Moving her legs and arms, Silvermist lazily made a snow fairy. Tink fluttered over to sit beside her.

"You'll have no problem making the diamond-dust snowflake now," Silvermist said to Tink.

"Yes, my snowflake will be beautiful," Tink said with a happy sigh. She reached into her sleeve for the crystal bottle. But it wasn't there.

Tink jumped to her feet and whirled around. The bottle lay several wingbeats away on its side in the snow. She flew to it. The cork had come out, and the bottle was empty!

Silvermist hurried over to Tink. All around her, the snow glittered in the sunlight. But was it snow, or was it diamond dust?

"Oh, Silvermist, what am I going to do?" Tink wailed.

One by one, the winter fairies came over to Tink and Silvermist. They looked sadly at the empty bottle and then at the glittering snow.

"Can't you sort out the diamond dust from the snow?" Silvermist asked their new friends.

The winter fairies frowned. "I don't think so," one said at last.

"I could use a magnet!" Tink shouted. But her determined look vanished when she realized that diamond dust, unlike the metals she usually worked with, wasn't magnetic.

But Tink's idea had gotten Silvermist thinking. Water fairies attracted water to themselves, just like magnets drew iron. And what was snow, after all, but frozen water?

If the winter fairies could melt the snow in the spot where Tink had spilled the dust, Silvermist would be able to pull the water away. Then Tink could collect the diamond dust.

It might not work, but they had to try.

Silvermist shared her idea with the winter fairies. She'd need their help to melt the snowflakes in this part of the clearing. Tink would have to gather the diamond dust quickly once Silvermist lifted the water away.

"Yes," one of the winter fairies said. She nodded eagerly as the idea sank in. "I think that would work!"

The winter fairies formed a circle around the spot where the bottle had fallen. In the centre of the circle, Tink fluttered beside Silvermist.

"Do you really think —" Tink started.

"We're going to try," Silvermist assured her with a small but hopeful smile.

The winter fairies linked hands and shut their eyes. Slowly, the snow at their feet began to melt. Silvermist raised her arms and drew the water upwards. As Tinker Bell watched, it lifted off the ground and whirled above their heads, a watery spiral of melted snow!

"Aha!" Tink cried. She dove towards the ground, which was now free of snow. The diamond dust sparkled as brightly as a lost gem. She swept up the pieces and funneled them back into the crystal bottle. Then she stuffed the cork firmly back in the bottle.

"She's done!" the water fairy called to the winter fairies. Suddenly Silvermist felt a shift in the air. As she watched, the water swirling above her head changed into thousands of little snowflakes. The snow fell on the fairies' upturned faces.

Tinker Bell and Silvermist thanked the winter fairies. Then they raced back to the meadow.

Tink vanished into her workshop for three days. At last she emerged. She flew straight to Silvermist. Diamond dust sparkled on her cheeks and in her hair.

"Look," she said in a whisper. She held out the diamond-dust snowflake. It glittered in the sunlight.

"Tink, it's beautiful!" Silvermist exclaimed.

Tink hugged Silvermist. "I couldn't have done it without you," she said. "The snowflake was your idea. You went with me to the woods. And you saved the lost diamond dust! This is your gift to the queen as much as it is mine."

That evening, Silvermist and Tinker Bell presented their gift to Queen Clarion.

"By the Second Star!" the queen exclaimed. "I've never seen such a snowflake. However did you make this?"

Tinker Bell smiled, then nudged Silvermist forwards. "With a little help from the best water-talent fairy in Pixie Hollow!" Tink cried.

Silvermist's heart skipped happily. How had she ever thought anything could be better than being a water-talent fairy? She had the best talent in the world!

The Perfect Painting

Bess whistled as she flew through the woods. The art-talent fairy was on her way to her studio. She couldn't wait to get started on a new painting.

"Where are you off to in such a hurry?" a voice called.

Bess paused in midair. Then she saw her friend Fira resting on a flower patch.

"To my studio!" Bess said. "I want to make the perfect painting to hang on the wall. Something that will inspire me every time I look at it."

"Good luck!" Fira replied. She waved as Bess zipped away.

"Where is Bess going?" someone asked.

Fira turned around and saw Rani walking towards her. "Bess is off to her studio," Fira said. "She needs some inspiration."

Rani gasped. "Bess isn't feeling inspired?"

"She is, but –" Fira began to explain.

But Rani wasn't listening. "I know just what she needs!" she said and hurried off.

Rani skipped along a path through the meadow. By the time she arrived at Havendish Stream, she was bursting with excitement.

As a water-talent fairy, Rani was always happiest when she was close to water. She knelt beside the stream and peered into it.

After a moment, Rani plucked a smooth stone from the water. "It's perfect!" she cried.

"What's perfect?" Tinker Bell asked, flying up behind her.

Rani grinned at her friend. "This!" she exclaimed, holding out the stone. "Fira says Bess needs some inspiration," Rani told Tink. "And I thought, what's more inspiring than a beautiful stone that has been worn smooth by the water? I can't wait for Bess to see it!" Rani said and skipped off.

"Inspiration?" Tink said to herself. Whenever she needed inspiration, she looked at a small silver bowl in her workshop. It had been her first repair as a tinker fairy in Never Land.

"That's it!" Tink cried. "I know just what Bess needs."

Moments later, Tinker Bell was on her way to Bess's studio. She was struggling to carry a large copper pot.

"Let me help you, Tink," her friend Lily, a garden talent, called. "Where are you taking that pot?"

Tink told the garden talent that she was bringing the pot to Bess for inspiration.

"My violets are very inspiring!" Lily exclaimed. "We can plant one of them in this pot."

The two fairies flew to Lily's garden. Lily chose her most beautiful flower and arranged it in the pot.

"Perfect!" Lily cried.

As Tink and Lily flew through the forest with the flowerpot, they spotted their friend Beck. The animal talent was sitting on a tree branch with a squirrel.

"Where are you going?" Beck called.

"To Bess's studio," Lily replied.

"Bess needs some inspiration right away!" Tink said.

"Did you hear that?" Beck asked the squirrel. "Bess is feeling uninspired."

The squirrel chattered and twitched his fluffy tail.

"Hmm," Beck replied. "I'm not saying a walnut isn't inspiring, but I have something else in mind."

Meanwhile, Bess finally arrived in the deepest part of the woods. Her art studio came into view and she smiled.

Bess's studio was a plain wooden crate that had once been used to hold tangerines. She had found it washed up on the shore of Never Land and had used magic to move it to a very quiet, peaceful part of the woods.

"There will be no interruptions here," Bess said as she flew into the studio. "I can paint in peace all day."

Bess sat down on her stool and stared at the white birch-bark paper. She held up her paintbrush and got ready to make the first stroke... but she couldn't decide what to paint!

"That's odd," Bess said to herself. Usually, she was overflowing with ideas for beautiful paintings. But today her mind was blank.

"Should I paint a flower?" she asked herself. "Or a tree? Or maybe a sunset?" All of those things sounded pretty, but none of them seemed quite right.

Bess sighed and frowned at her easel. She hovered upside down, hoping that would give her an idea. But it just made her dizzy.

"Why don't I feel inspired?" Bess said as she righted herself.

Above her, the leaves rustled in the breeze. The art talent scowled up at them. "Shh!" she whispered. "I need peace and quiet to concentrate."

A bird chirped from a nearby branch. That gave Bess an idea. "Maybe if I sing something," she mused. She launched into the first verse of her favourite song, but her voice soon trailed off. She felt very silly singing to an easel.

Bess tried meditating, yelling, reciting fairy history, covering her eyes with a fern, counting to one hundred and pretending not to care. Nothing worked.

"Oh!" Bess cried. "Why can't I think of anything?"

Finally, Bess fell flat on her back. She stared up at the ceiling.

"I'm not going to move until I get an idea for the perfect painting," she said firmly. "I mean it. I don't care if it takes the whole afternoon."

"Knock, knock!"

Bess turned and saw Fira approaching the studio.

"I wanted to see how your painting was going," Fira said. She peered strangely at Bess. "Why are you lying on the floor?"

"I was just thinking about what to paint," Bess said, climbing to her feet and dusting herself off.

"You haven't started yet?" Fira asked. "What happened?"

"Well..." Bess said, feeling embarrassed.

"Bess!" Tink called out. She and Lily flew towards the studio with their flowerpot. "We brought you some inspiration!"

"Me too!" Rani cried. She stepped into the clearing, followed by Beck.

Bess looked at her friends and their gifts. Tink's copper pot was so shiny, and Lily's violet was the prettiest purple she'd ever seen. The river stone Rani held was as smooth and blue as the water in Havendish Stream. Beck had brought two halves of a speckled egg, which would be great for mixing paint in. Her friends were so thoughtful.

"That's it!" Bess cried.

Bess grabbed her largest brush and darted to the longest wall in her studio. She painted as fast as she could. The other fairies watched quietly while she worked.

Finally, Bess stood back to admire her painting. She had created a picture of her friends. She smiled as she turned to look at them.

"What do you think?" Bess asked.

"It's beautiful," Lily said with a happy sigh.

"I wanted to paint the perfect picture to inspire me while I

work every day," Bess said. "And as soon as you all showed up, I realized that —"

"Nothing is more inspiring than good friends!" Rani exclaimed.